W9-AYW-508

Kicked Out

Beth Goobie

orca soundings

ORCA BOOK PUBLISHERS

Text copyright © 2002 BETH GOOOBIE

All rights reserved. No part of this publication may be reproduced or transmitted
any form or by any means, electronic or mechanical, including photocopying,
recording or by any information storage and retrieval system now known or to be
invented, without permission in writing from the publisher.

Library and Archives Canada Cataloguing in Publication

Goobie, Beth, 1959-

Kicked out

(Orca soundings)

ISBN 1-55143-244-7

I. Title. II. Series.

PS8563.O8326K53 2002   jC813'.54   C2002-910695-8
PZ7.G597Ki 2002

First published in the United States, 2002
Library of Congress Control Number: 2002107489

Summary: Dime can't get along with her parents. When she moves in with her old
brother, she finds out that if she starts believing in herself, other people will too.

Orca Book Publishers gratefully acknowledges the support for its publishing
programs provided by the following agencies: the Government of Canada through
the Book Publishing Industry Development Program and the Canada Council for the
Arts, and the Province of British Columbia through the BC Arts Council
and the Book Publishing Tax Credit.

Design and typesetting by Christine Toller
Cover photography by Eyewire

ORCA BOOK PUBLISHERS
PO Box 5626, STN. B
VICTORIA, BC CANADA
V8R 6S4

ORCA BOOK PUBLISHERS
PO Box 468
CUSTER, WA USA
98240-0468

www.orcabook.com
Printed and bound in Canada.

010 09 08 07 • 7 6 5 4

for Claude

Chapter One

It was another one of those face-the-music moments. Yelling parents — they make heavy metal sound like a fairy tale. With a sigh, I slid off the back of Gabe's street bike and took off my helmet. I handed it to him and he hooked it onto the bike, a Kawasaki Ninja. I was glad he kept the motor running. It was after midnight, and I wanted everyone in Winnipeg to see this. Here I was, coming back from a date with Gabe Jordan — the cutest guy in the West. Finally, he'd dumped his old girlfriend and picked up me. I hoped my parents were hiding behind the living room curtains, getting a good eyeball.

We set a world record for the longest kiss. Then Gabe said into my ear, "Call me tomorrow, Dime."

I stood and watched him roar off down the street. Now everyone in the neighborhood would know about my love life. Tomorrow morning the phone lines would be buzzing with gossip. Mom would be so embarrassed. I grinned, thinking about it. At the same time, my stomach bunched into a tight sore lump. I wished I was driving Gabe's Ninja — down the street and on into forever. But no, Gabe got to disappear. I had to go inside and deal with the Two-Headed Monster that was my parents.

First things first — I took out my nose ring. Mom thinks only drug dealers wear nose rings. Last time she saw me wearing it, she said I was grounded until I grew up. I never paid any attention to the grounding — I didn't have time to waste, sitting around the house.

But I did stop wearing my nose ring at home. Life is a lot easier if a parent isn't blocking the door when you want to go out.

As I went up the front walk, I got ready for battle. I made my eyes look really bored and pulled my mouth into a pout. I was really good at this — I'd spent hours practicing in front of my bedroom mirror. Looking bored was my best defense. It drove my parents crazy, and then they gave up on whatever argument we were having.

Slowly, I pulled open the front door. Arms crossed, Mom stood in the front hall wearing her Terminator face.

"Just where have you been?" she asked.

"Out," I said. I pulled off my jacket and hung it up.

It was always *Die Hard III* in our house, only the weapons were our mouths. Dad appeared behind Mom, on Info-Search.

"Out where?" he asked.

I kicked off my boots and started to push past them. Dad took my shoulders in his

3

hands — not hard, just enough to keep me there. Then he yelled, "You were supposed to be home at nine."

"So, did you call the cops?" I asked.

Fifteen years old and I had to be in at nine. It was ridiculous. To make things worse, when I came in late, Dad would start yelling. I'd put on my extra-bored face, and he'd yell even louder. Sometimes he got to me. My defense system would crumble and I'd go nuclear. I hated it when I yelled back, but I often ended up doing it.

"This is our house and we make the rules, Dime. If we say you're home at nine, that's when you walk in the door! No excuses!" Dad shouted.

Their house, not mine. For a moment, my eyes burned, and I thought I was about to cry. Then I got it under control. I slid a smile over my mouth and looked him straight in the eye.

"Make me," I said softly.

He looked as if he might hit me. Then he roared, "No respect! You've got no respect for your parents or anyone else. We work hard to put food on the table. You're out there blowing your mind on drugs. Flunking school. Dressed like you're in a street gang. Look at your hair. And you're running around with some guy twice your age."

Gabe is seventeen. My parents seriously needed to get real. I took a deep breath and started arguing back.

"I'm almost sixteen! You treat me like I'm twelve. My friends don't have to be in until midnight on Fridays," I said, still trying to keep cool.

"You used to be such a sweet little girl. How did you turn into such a problem?" Mom moaned.

"I dunno. Maybe it's all those drugs you say I'm taking," I shrugged. As a matter of fact, I didn't do drugs, but sometimes they made me want to.

"Your brother never did this to us," Dad said.

"If only you could be a little more like him," Mom added.

That did it. If I didn't get out of there that minute, I'd start yelling. Then I'd break

5

down and cry in front of them. I couldn't do that, couldn't let them see they'd gotten to me. I pushed past them and ran upstairs to my room. I slammed the door and locked it — my door-slamming habit started when I was nine. I dove onto my bed and buried my face in my stuffed rabbit. A wild pounding filled my ears, and I counted heartbeats. Slowly my heart grew quiet, and I could hear my parents' voices blending with the TV.

I was starting to feel guilty about the look on Mom's face. It was always there these days. It was as if she looked at me and she started to hurt. I didn't want that. I wanted Mom to see me and smile, but it never seemed to work that way. There was just endless yelling and hurt. Maybe I should have crawled into the nearest Dumpster instead of coming home. *Curled up with everyone's junk where I belonged.* That was what I was thinking when I finally fell asleep.

It was late when I woke up the next morning. I was still wearing my Metallica T-shirt from last night, and my hair looked like an old broom. I decided to add some ripped jeans and drag myself down for breakfast. I didn't bother washing up. That would show them they hadn't gotten to me. None of their yelling had changed a thing.

As I came downstairs, I could hear Dad's voice in the kitchen. He was saying, "I tell you, we don't know what to do with her anymore. It's as if she wants to hurt us every way she can."

I stopped and swallowed. Why didn't they just buy me a T-shirt with *Problem Child* printed across it? I could put it on every morning when I got up. They wouldn't have to bother talking to me anymore, and I could wear their opinion wherever I went.

I heard a voice. My brother Darren said, "Give her a break. She's working things out."

"You were never like that," Mom said.

"What's that got to do with it?" Darren asked.

"We just want her to succeed in life. Right now, she's a failure at everything," said Dad.

I went stiff. I wasn't even in the same room with them yet, and I was ready to yell.

"Dime is not a failure. She's just a little different than I am," said Darren.

"That's the problem," said Dad.

I'd heard enough. I walked in, running a hand through my hair. Last month I'd dyed part of it pink. It looked good with my green eyes. Since my hair is so short, it sticks up in the morning until I wet it down. My parents thought I had a Mohawk.

I made my voice very loud and said, "Morning, Darren."

"Morning, Sis," he said.

There was only silence from my parents. Their mouths had died. Well, that was fine with me. I picked up Darren's toast and took a bite, then gave him a jam kiss on his cheek.

"New chair? You get the Rick Hansen model?" I asked. Darren had been a quad for about three years. He'd broken his neck when he was eighteen.

Darren grinned and said, "Around the world in forty days."

Darren's chair may have been cool, but his matching sweatshirt and pants were definitely a problem. They were almost as bad as the sweat suits my parents had on. Darren was an okay guy, but he needed fashion advice really bad. He was twenty-one going on fifty.

I dropped some bread into the toaster. Then I poured a coffee and took a loud slurp. I looked at Darren and said, "Gabe's teaching me to drive his Ninja. When I turn sixteen in June, I'm going to get my license."

Mom dropped her fork. Dad pushed back his chair. I knew this would set them off, but I figured Darren would protect me from the fireworks. Dad went straight into a dead roar.

"I won't allow it!" he shouted.

"Oh Dime, what next?" Mom groaned.

I shrugged and said, "I dunno — AIDS?"

Dad put both hands over his face and sat quietly. That surprised me. Why did they always take everything so seriously? I looked

9

at Darren and lifted an eyebrow. Then he surprised me too.

"I don't think AIDS is funny, Dime," he said.

"Okay." Now I was going red. As usual, everything was horrible because I was there. I took another loud slurp of my coffee.

"We've been talking about you moving in with me," Darren said.

"For real?" I gasped.

I glanced at Mom and Dad. They were both staring silently at the table.

"What do you think?" Darren asked.

"Tell me when!" I was grinning ear to ear.

"Like now. Today," Darren said.

I put down my coffee and answered without thinking twice. "I'm packing!" I said.

"You'll have to cook," Darren warned.

"It's a deal," I grinned and kissed him on my way out of the kitchen.

I didn't look at either of my parents.

Chapter Two

When I got to my room, I started throwing stuff into garbage bags. I wanted to be out of the house before my parents could change their minds. When I really want to clean out a room, things can disappear fast. I shoved my stuffed rabbit, some CDs, underwear and my cowboy boots into the same bag. Then I picked up my photo album.

Something made me stop what I was

doing and flip through it. There were the family pictures from our trip to Niagara Falls and Ottawa when I was eleven. We sure knew how to smile for the camera. It was the only time we looked as if we liked each other. But that trip had been before Darren had broken his neck. We'd all gotten along better back then. I flipped to the front page of the photo album and smiled. It had my favorite picture — one of me laughing with Dad when I was five. Back then, we'd lived in a small town near Winnipeg called Gimli.

Then came the pictures of Darren in the hospital as he recovered. He'd been flown to Winnipeg. My parents had camped out in the hospital parking lot in our motor home for seven weeks. They'd been with him every day. I'd stayed with my grandparents, even though I was the one who'd gone through the car crash with him.

I decided to take the photo album with me. I'd keep it somewhere out of sight, like under the bed. Before I went downstairs, I pushed open my bedroom window and gave a Tarzan yell. Then I dragged my three garbage bags out the front door and down the ramp. Dad had built one at each door for Darren's chair. I put the bags in the back of Darren's van, then walked back into the house. What would saying goodbye be like? A funeral? A boxing match?

It turned out to be another two-mouth lecture.

"You listen to your brother and don't give him any trouble," Mom said.

"I don't want to hear about you coming in at all hours," Dad said.

"You make sure you cook the food Darren likes. Not hamburgers all the time for yourself," Mom got in.

"And do your homework. It's about time you passed something," Dad added.

"Yeah, bye," I said. It felt like time to get out of there.

Mom gave Darren a kiss. Dad told him, "Take care of yourself."

At the door, I thought all I was going to get was The Glare. Then Mom sort of moaned and gave me a hug. I've always liked hugs from Mom. She smelled nice and it made me feel like her little kid again. It was about the only time, for a couple of seconds, that we got along. I hugged her back quickly, then let go. Dad just looked at me and shook his head as if he was dizzy ... or out of it.

"I'll pass every class — you'll see," I told him. Then I climbed into the passenger seat of Darren's van.

Darren got himself settled behind the wheel and we drove off. *Freedom*, I thought, and put my nose ring back in. Just to let Darren know he wasn't going to run my life either.

"Dad and I cleaned out my study for your bedroom," Darren said as he drove along Portage Avenue.

"When was this?" I asked, going stiff.

"A couple of weeks ago. We've been talking about this for a while," he said.

So everyone had known about this except me. Why hadn't they included me in their little chats about my life plans? I chewed my lip and stared out the window. I thought I'd left my parents behind, but it looked like they were still all over my life. Then I decided not to get angry. It made sense that Dad would have cleaned out the room for me. After all, Darren couldn't do it alone.

Darren turned down Sherburn Street and his apartment block came into view. It had been specially adapted for wheelchairs. Darren turned into his parking space and we sat quietly for a moment. Finally he said, "They're afraid for you, Dime."

"Afraid *of* me, you mean. Afraid of me and my friends," I said.

"Maybe," Darren said.

As soon as I dropped my garbage bags inside the front door, I headed for the phone. I had to call Gabe right away and let him know my new number. My phone call dragged him out of bed, but he was still chipper. Of course, he said he'd be right over to see my new place. Then I phoned my best friend Tiff. She said the same thing.

After the calls, I followed Darren down the hall, dragging my bags of stuff. I felt a little guilty about taking his extra room — he could use the space. He's studying engineering at the University of Manitoba. He gets really high marks, which sort of makes up for my D's and C's. Well, and the odd E.

Except for a bed, a dresser and Darren's desk, the room was empty. The first thing I did was put a sign on my door: DIME'S ROOM. KEEP OUT. A lot of people wonder about my nickname. One day when I was eight, I refused to come out of my room when I was called. Playing Barbies seemed more important than whatever Mom wanted me to do. When she asked why I hadn't answered, I told her I didn't like my name. So she asked me what I'd like to be called. It was a day I felt as if I was worth about ten cents, so I said, "Dime." No one asked why, and the nickname stuck. So did the feeling.

I changed my Metallica T-shirt and started to unpack. I was just setting my stuffed rabbit onto the bed when the door buzzer rang. I ran to the apartment door and opened it. There stood my boyfriend and my best friend, grinning at me.

"Darren, these are my friends Gabe and Tiff," I said. That was when I realized I'd forgotten to ask Darren if they could come over. Oh well, it was my apartment too.

"Hey, great chair! Sometime I'll race you on my bike," Gabe said, going over to the fridge.

Tiff laughed, but Darren's face went blank. Stupid jokes about my brother's wheelchair make me want to punch someone. But you can't punch your boyfriend, especially if his ex is still hot on his trail. I shrugged at Darren and he rolled his eyes.

"Hey, see anything in there to eat? I'm starved," Tiff said, sitting down at the kitchen table.

My friends were embarrassing me. They wouldn't have done this at my parents' place — not that I could ever have them over much. Why were they acting like this here?

"There's some pop," Darren said.

"How 'bout this pizza?" Gabe asked, opening the freezer.

"That's for Dime and me," Darren said.

"But we're dying of hunger right here in front of you!" Tiff wailed.

I stepped in and said, "Here — suck on this sugar cube. It'll bring you back to life."

I shoved the bowl of sugar cubes at her. Then I pulled the pop out of the fridge and closed the door.

"Let's sit down," I said.

Darren joined us at the table. Gabe grinned at him and said, "Hey, man — you don't need a regular chair."

"No, I've sort of got one stuck to my body," Darren said.

"So, how are you going to drink your pop?" Gabe asked.

"The same way you do — down my throat," Darren said.

Why couldn't they just drink their pop and shut up? Or talk about the weather? Gabe kept staring at Darren's fingers. My brother's hands look unusual because of the way he uses them. After the accident, he couldn't move his finger muscles. That made his hands curl up. Now he holds things between his palms. At first he couldn't even lift his arms. The doctors told him he'd never be able to, but Darren surprised them.

"How d'you get the can up to your mouth? D'you need help?" Gabe asked.

Even Tiff looked uncomfortable. "Gabe, you're being a dork," she said.

"Hey — a stereo!" Gabe said quickly and stood up. I could tell he was embarrassed and wanted to change the subject. He crouched down in front of Darren's stereo and turned it full blast. Then he came back to the table and yelled, "This is great!"

Darren didn't look at me, but I could feel him sizing up the situation. He picked up his pop and drank it, not seeming to notice the way Gabe stared.

"You're a real pro!" Gabe yelled at him. The music was so loud, we were all yelling. If Darren hadn't been there, I would have been having fun. But something in his face kept me from laughing at Gabe's jokes. Instead, my brother was making me think about what Gabe was actually saying. Was Gabe having a sub-zero day, or did he always sound like this?

Darren waited for a break in the music, then said, "I'm going to study."

He stopped by the stereo and turned the volume down. Then he disappeared into his bedroom. Right away, Gabe went over and turned the volume back up.

"Gabe! He has to study," I said, getting up.

Gabe pulled my face to his and kissed me. "You're beautiful," he said.

This kind of took my mind off the stereo. In fact, it made me want to turn it up more. Then the door buzzer went again. I could hardly hear it over the music. I waited for Darren to answer it. When he didn't, I pulled myself out of Gabe's hug and opened the door.

"Hello," I said.

The woman standing in the hall was about Mom's age. She had that Mom Look on her face. Right away she started yelling, but then she had to because of the music.

"I'm the landlady here! What d'you think you're doing with all that noise? This is a nice quiet building. No one who makes a lot of noise stays here for long!" she shouted.

"Sorry!" I yelled back.

Behind me, the noise suddenly cut off. I turned around to see Gabe standing by the stereo and grinning at us.

"Hey, we were just leaving," he said.

"And don't come back," the woman snapped and walked away.

Gabe shrugged and said, "Guess we were giving her a little headache."

Tiff snorted and stood up. She and Gabe came over to the door.

"Coming with us, babe?" Gabe said into my ear.

"I should ask Darren," I said. I wondered what my brother was thinking about all of this.

"Hey, you're on your own now, right? And it's a Saturday," Gabe said.

Gabe is so gorgeous. How was I supposed to say I should do my homework with his mouth one inch from mine?

"I want you to," Gabe said softly.

Unpacking could wait. I slid Darren's extra key off the hook and walked out.

Chapter Three

I got in late and Darren was asleep. I hadn't made the bed yet, so I ended up sleeping in my clothes. When I woke, it tasted as if something really ugly had crawled into my mouth. I dragged myself to the bathroom and started to brush my teeth. Then I realized I was using Darren's comb. This was definitely going to be a problem day.

Darren's aide had already come and

gone. Someone comes in every morning to help him get up and going. Usually the aide also made meals, but as of yesterday, that was my job. Only I hadn't been here last night to cook supper. Suddenly I wondered what Darren had eaten. I felt so bad, I wanted to blend in with the wall and stay there forever. Slowly, I walked into the kitchen. There Darren sat, reading the newspaper and drinking a coffee the aide must have made for him.

"Sorry about last night. What did you eat?" I asked.

"I cooked the pizza. Took a while, but I managed," Darren said, not looking up. More and more, I wanted to become part of a wall. Any wall would do.

"And I'm sorry about being late with your breakfast," I added softly.

Darren gave me a sideways smile. "So, how's life with my new roommate?"

I dug in for a lecture about getting in late, but Darren went back to the newspaper. I smiled and said, "Ready to make your breakfast. Eggs?"

"Two, please. There's some bacon. And could you throw in some toast?" Darren asked.

"Cooking for you is going to be a full-time job," I groaned. Darren read while I cooked. I loved the smell of bacon and eggs frying, but Mom had always made them for me. I tried to remember how she poured in the oil and waited for it to heat up. I almost had my nose in the frying pan, I was watching everything so closely. I chewed on my lip and hoped nothing would burn. But the food looked pretty normal when I set our plates on the table.

"This is great," said Darren after the first bite. I figured he was probably lying, but I still beamed.

"You going to work out?" I asked.

"I might. You going to unpack?" Darren asked.

I got stiff. I couldn't help it. I was so used to Mom and Dad wanting to know about every minute of my day. I stabbed at my eggs and said, "Maybe I like my room the way it is."

"It's your room. I do need to talk to you about something though," Darren said.

"What?" I sighed loudly. So this was it — Showdown Number One.

"Dime, you look like I've got a gun to your head. Relax, okay? We just need to figure out how we can live together," said Darren. He smiled, but my stomach had gone through a change of state — from stomach to rock.

"You mean rules. Your rules. You just want to figure out how to control me," I snapped. I didn't like my voice sharp as a knife, but I couldn't help it.

Darren looked surprised. With a small frown, he said, "No, not control. Dime, we're sharing the same space. We're bound to bump into each other. I thought we could discuss what you like and what I like. That way we can figure out how to make it all work."

My arms were crossed over my chest. I tried to get them uncrossed, but they felt stuck. *I* felt stuck, as if I was glued to a bad attitude I couldn't get rid of. I knew Darren was different from my parents, but right then he felt the same to me. It felt as if he was telling me: *This is the way you comb your hair. This is the way you tie your shoes. This is the way you brush your teeth.*

"I'm old enough to live my own life. No rules," I muttered.

"That's a rule," Darren said.

I stared down at my plate. He was right. It looked as if you just couldn't get away from them.

"Why are you mad at me?" Darren asked, his voice soft.

I looked at him in surprise. Then I shook my head and said, "I'm not."

I could see he was thinking about me pretty hard. It made me nervous.

"Yes, you are," Darren said quietly.

That was when the phone rang. I picked it up to find Mom on the other end.

"Dime?" she yelled. Her voice was so loud, she just about took out my ear. One word and she was already in full combat mode.

"Yeah?" I said. I was trying to keep cool. It felt as if she was right in my face.

"Where were you last night? When I called at 10 p.m., Darren said you weren't available. I know what that means where you're concerned, young lady. If this doesn't work out with Darren, you'll come straight back home. I'm not letting you ruin his life," yelled Mom. She sounded ready to lecture me for about a week.

"Mom, you sound like I've got a gun to your head. Relax," I said, giving Darren a grin. He grinned back.

"You listen to what your brother says," Mom said, as if I hadn't said anything.

"Yup. Gotta go. Want to talk to Darren?" I asked, but I didn't wait for her answer. I could hear her calling my name as I handed the phone over to Darren.

I showered and changed. When I came out of the bedroom, I put the dishes in the dishwasher. Mom finally let Darren off the phone just as the door buzzer rang.

"Oh, that's Gabe. I've got a driving lesson," I said. I grabbed my jacket.

"When will you unpack?" asked Darren.

"I dunno. I'll be back to make your lunch. Promise," I said, kissing his cheek.

The apartment hallway stretched ahead of me, quiet and empty. I was free to go any-where I wanted— no parents, no problems. Life felt great, and it felt even greater when I got outside. There was Gabe, sitting on his bike by the curb. One glimpse of him and that wave pool feeling rippled through me. Gabe was so gorgeous. I just couldn't figure out why he wanted to hang around with me.

"Hey, Dime," he said.

I kissed him. That took quite a while. Then I put on the helmet he gave me and got on behind him. As we rode down Henderson Highway, I thought, *See, Gabe doesn't try to run my life. He's just a great kisser, that's all.*

When we got out of Winnipeg and onto a quiet road, Gabe stopped. I got into the driver's position. Gabe liked this. I had to keep my hands on the handle-grips and he had to keep his hands on me. It was fun, but it made it hard to concentrate. I listened to him point out the different bumps and knobs on the dash. I knew they were important, but he had his chin on my shoulder. He was sort of breathing onto my cheek. I didn't want to flunk out here — not on a Kawasaki Ninja. I tried repeating the information back to him.

"No, no, no, Dime. You've got it all wrong. Weren't you listening?" Gabe asked.

I went stiff. I hate it when someone says "no" more than once. Like, I got it the first time, right?

"Lucky I'm checking to make sure I have it right, huh?" I grinned.

"I'll explain it again," Gabe sighed.

He had to explain everything, right down to how the nuts and bolts fit together. But he made it sound so complicated. By the time he was done, it felt like it would be easier to fly a supersonic jet. Finally, he settled back and said, "Go for it."

As I hit the starter button, I was chewing my lip. I had to get this right. I'd gotten most of it, but I had a habit of forgetting the most important parts. Like lighting the Bunsen burner *before* starting a science experiment. Like turning off the stove element *after* boiling water for tea. I get nervous around people and it makes my mind fall apart. I can cover pretty well — no one expects a kid who looks tough to scare easy. I bet my parents never guessed how bad I shook after our fights. I'd go sit on my bed, hold my stuffed rabbit, and just shake and shake. Whenever I saw that *look* on their faces — the one that went with the one-hundred-and-one questions — the shaking always started. But I never let them see it. I kept it deep inside, then took it up to my room and let it loose.

But this morning, things were going pretty well. Everything seemed to be under control. I was sitting in the driver's position, with Gabe hanging on behind me. We roared by farmhouses with dogs barking in the driveways. I even passed several carloads of dressed-up families coming back from church. Then I saw a stop sign ahead. Just beyond it, cars were zooming past. It looked like we were headed straight for a major road.

Stop, I thought. *I've got to stop. How do I stop this thing?*

Suddenly all the knobs looked like something out of a sci-fi movie. It was as if I'd never seen them before.

I can't do it. I'm gonna mess up. Gabe will hate me, I thought.

I blanked out. My brain shattered into a thousand pieces and flew away.

"Brake! Brake! Brake!" Gabe kept yelling. He started slamming his helmet against the back of mine to get me to wake up. Finally something clicked, and I remembered. We stopped just on the edge of the major road. A car whizzed by.

Gabe doesn't worry too much about causing a scene. He got off, hopping mad and yelling, "Get off my bike! Get off my bike! You're crazy, nuts or just plain stupid! You got some kind of a death wish?"

I slid off the bike and watched him climb on. He yelled some more, then kicked the starter and roared off down the highway. It got really quiet. As I stood there alone, the shaking started. I sat down with my back to the stop sign and took off my helmet. I didn't have my stuffed rabbit, so I hugged myself. I kept hearing different voices in my head — Mom's, Dad's and Gabe's. They were all yelling *Stupid! Crazy! No good! Death wish!* Their voices kept getting louder and louder, mixing together until my head hurt. I told myself I wasn't going to cry. I wasn't going to let it hurt. I was going to get up and walk all the way back to Winnipeg. I'd show Gabe I didn't need him. I didn't need him or my parents or anyone.

That's when I heard the roar of the motorcycle. Relief hit me so hard, I did start to cry then. Gabe wasn't going to leave me alone. He was coming back to get me. Maybe I was stupid and a no-good nutcase, but he still liked me.

I wiped my eyes and hoped my

makeup hadn't smeared. Gabe stopped in front of me. He took off his helmet.

"Hey, babe, going my way?" he grinned weakly.

I stared at my feet and said, "Sorry. I guess I blew it."

"I'll get over it. C'mon, get on," he said.

We kissed and made up. Then we rode back, me hanging onto him pretty tight. I was relieved we were okay. Still, something in me kept saying, *He took off and left me alone out there. Why didn't he say he was sorry?*

Chapter Four

When I got back, I started lunch. I decided to make Kraft Dinner and hot dogs. I'm not much of a cook — my specialty is boiled eggs. That's as good as it gets. Reading the wiener package, I got nervous. There were no instructions.

"Darren, when you make hot dogs, do you boil the water and then drop in the wieners? Or do you put the wieners in cold water first and then boil them?" I asked.

"I dunno," said Darren, looking puzzled. We started to laugh.

"I guess I'll just wing it," I said nervously.

Darren got out his books and started studying at the kitchen table. This made me more nervous. I wanted him to go into his bedroom where he wouldn't see any mistakes I made. But it was his apartment. So I fussed around the stove, watching everything carefully and hoping he'd keep quiet if anything blew up. To my surprise, nothing went wrong. The wieners cooked and the noodles boiled as if they did this every day. It was only after I'd set everything on the table that I noticed how relaxed I was. Then I realized why. Darren hadn't yelled at me. He hadn't put me down once. My eyes stung and I blinked fast.

"What's the matter?" Darren asked.

"I like it here," I said.

He smiled and said, "I like you being here, too. And while you're here, could you get me a beer? It goes great with Kraft Dinner."

"Sure," I grinned and almost skipped to the fridge. I set the beer on the table next to Darren's hand. He leaned over and opened the bottle with his teeth.

"No hands," he grinned. His teeth are chipped from doing this, but no one can talk sense into him.

"You look like such a mild-mannered quad," I said.

"Super Quad," he said.

That afternoon, I unpacked. Darren headed off to the gym to work out, so the apartment was quiet. Times like this, I get to thinking about the accident. It happened when Darren and I were coming back from an all-night curling bonspiel. I was asleep in the back seat. It was still dark, and Darren ran into a moose that had walked onto the road. The moose came through the windshield, and the car rolled into a field. I was unconscious for a while. When I came to, I found Darren still in his seat, twisted up funny. His face and arms were cut up, so there was blood. I sat there holding his hand, then ran to the road when I heard a car coming. It was at least another hour before the ambulance arrived. Sometimes I feel as if I'm still sitting there in the dark, hoping and praying my brother will live.

Of course, he did live. We found out that he'd broken his neck, but not his glasses. Darren seemed to be the only person in our family who didn't change after that. He went through the rehab program and learned to hold a spoon with the Universal Cuff. Slowly, he got back some use of his hands so he could hold things with his palms. He started university and learned to drive a van with touch controls. Sometimes it seems like he went on as if the accident never happened.

Thinking about it, I started banging things around in my room. How could Darren just pick up and go on living? For me, it felt as if there was still a bad accident waiting around every corner. And when my parents looked at me, I knew what they were thinking. *You've always been a problem, Dime. You were already a failure. It should have been your neck that was broken, not our boy's.*

Of course, they never said any of this out loud. In our family, we don't talk about things — we yell. Or we look at each other and think things loudly inside our heads.

That evening was sort of peaceful. When Mom called, Darren handled her call. Gabe called a little later, and I handled him. I made hamburgers and even got some studying done. That night, I lay awake in bed, thinking about the evening. There had been no arguments, no yelling, no putdowns. Did it ever make me feel different. It helped me sleep, too. The next morning, as I stood at the bus stop with Tiff, I actually felt awake. This was something new for me — mornings look a lot better after nine hours of sleep.

We got to school with fifteen minutes to spare and headed for the student parking area. Right away I saw Gabe on his bike, talking to kids sitting on the curb. I swung on behind him and wrapped my arms around his waist.

"Morning," I said. Everyone watched us. At our school, a lot of action went on around Gabe's Ninja.

"Hey, Gabe," said Tiff, leaning over the front of his bike.

"Yeah?" Gabe asked, but he was more interested in playing with the hole in the left knee of my jeans.

"Isn't that your ex over there?" Tiff asked, pointing.

I glanced toward the door. Our school has a different entrance for each social group. There's one for the preppies, the jocks, the skaters, and the headbangers. Gabe's ex was standing in the headbangers' entrance, wearing a tight Megadeth T-shirt. She was glaring at me as if she was planning the rest of my life. It looked short.

"Yeah, that's her," said Gabe. He grinned and started kissing me.

"Uh, Dime?" said Tiff.

"Yeah?" I asked. It was hard to concentrate on what she was saying. Gabe's a good kisser.

"I hear she's decided to remove half of your face," Tiff said.

I put my hand over Gabe's mouth and asked, "When did you hear this?"

"Last week, but it slipped my mind," Tiff said.

"Yeah, I heard about it too. Don't worry. She's a big talker," Gabe said.

"Thanks for telling me, you guys," I muttered. Gabe's ex was a good fighter. She picked most of her fights in the girls' bathrooms. "Queen of the Cans" was one of her nicer nicknames.

"Hey, don't worry about it — I'll protect you," Gabe said. He seemed pretty chipper about the whole thing.

"You going to walk into the girls' can with me?" I asked.

"Sure!" He looked enthusiastic.

The bell rang and everyone started to move. I noticed the ex was gone, so Gabe and I gave each other a long goodbye.

"Skip third period and come for a ride?" Gabe asked. He had a spare that class. I kissed him one last time.

"Bummer, but I can't. I've got a test in math," I sighed.

I took off into the school in a floating run, but I came down fast. When I rounded the last corner before my locker, there was Gabe's ex leaning against the wall.

I hadn't brushed up on any kung fu lately. Luckily, she was looking the other way. I backed up around the corner. Then I took the long way around to my homeroom. I was going to have to go to science class without my books. They were in my locker. If I tried to get them now, my class would be using my body for its next experiment.

Chapter Five

I've been in a couple of fights. I remember dragging a neighbor boy around by the hair in Grade 5. He'd shot one too many spitballs at me. From that point on, he took aim at other kids. Somehow, I couldn't see the same thing happening with the ex. She could have downed Mike Tyson — without gloves.

At mid-morning break, Tiff scouted out a safe bathroom for me to use. Then she stood guard at the door. While I was washing my hands, a girl came out of one of the stalls. She looked at me and said, "I hear there's a fight in the back parking lot at lunch. You're in it."

I pulled a bored look across my face. Without blinking, I said, "News to me."

"Better watch out. Her fingernails are switchblades," the girl laughed.

"Yeah? She'll probably chew them off worrying about me," I said.

The girl shrugged. Just before she walked out, she looked back and said, "I hear Gabe's the referee."

I looked at Tiff, who started drawing circles on the wall. I knew she was thinking about the same thing as me — Gabe's grin that morning when he'd seen his ex.

"You hear about any of this?" I asked.

Tiff twisted herself around inside her clothes and stared up at the ceiling. Finally, she said, "Maybe. But I know Gabe really likes you. He wouldn't let anything bad happen to you. I wouldn't worry about it."

Great — my best friend hadn't even bothered to tell me I was in danger of going extinct.

"Gabe's ex always goes for the face. I'm no Cover Girl, but this face is the only one I've got," I snapped.

"You could switch schools," Tiff said helpfully.

"I want to switch lives — with anyone. I'd even switch lives with my brother," I said.

Tiff stared at me, but I meant what I'd said. I would have given anything to be Darren. I'd wanted that all my life.

"Ah, c'mon, Dime — it'll be okay," Tiff said.

The bathroom was starting to feel like a danger zone. I'd been standing there too long, and Gabe's ex was bound to show up soon. I picked up my books and said, "Let's get out of here."

At lunchtime, I hid in a back corner of the library. I needed time to think, and I didn't want to see anyone. I figured the library was the one place my friends wouldn't come looking for me — not even Tiff. But the rumors did. Kids hung over the top of my study carrel, bugging me.

"Hey, Dime — ready for the rumble?" asked a preppie.

"Better pull that nose ring out. It's the first thing she'll go for," teased a skater.

When I walked out of the school that afternoon, I decided to use the preppie door. I knew the ex wouldn't go anywhere near there. It was pretty embarrassing, and the preppies sure had a lot to say about it.

"Hey, headbanger, use your own door," called a guy.

"Who dresses you — the Terminator?" asked his girlfriend.

"Don't be a man, girl. Don't be a man," said another guy.

"She's not a man. She's a sweet thing running from the Queen of the Cans. I hear she's about to get wasted," said an absolute nerd.

Normally, I wouldn't have let them get away with this kind of garbage. But today

I had better things to do than stand around wising up preps. I pushed my way down the crowded steps, getting comments the whole way. As I walked along the street, Gabe's bike came up beside me.

"Want a ride?" he grinned.

I wasn't sure. If this guy really liked me, why didn't he tell the ex to get lost? But if he really liked the ex, would he offer me a ride? Maybe he hadn't heard the rumors. The stuff about him as referee had to be bull. Gabe liked to watch boxing and wrestling, but who didn't? That didn't mean he'd stoop to setting up a fight between his girlfriend and his ex.

Besides, kids were watching. Everywhere I looked, they were turning around to stare. So I gave Gabe the same smile I gave my parents when they bugged me. I didn't mean to use it with Gabe — it just sort of showed up on my face. But Gabe didn't seem to notice anything strange.

"Going my way?" he asked.

"You bet," I said.

We took off and rode for a long time.

My arms were around him, and I could feel him breathing, solid and real. I knew then that what I'd been thinking was wrong. Gabe was mine, and no rumors or silly comments could ever take him away. I leaned my head on his back and watched everything go by. *Take me away from my life, Gabe*, I thought.

He didn't, of course. And he didn't explain his ex and the rumors, either. So when he dropped me off at Darren's apartment, I asked about it.

"You don't still like her, do you?" I said between kisses.

"No, no, no — it's all over with her," he mumbled.

"Does she know that?" I asked.

"Haven't I made it obvious?" sighed Gabe.

"So why does she want to fight me, then?" I asked.

"She's just jealous. She won't go through with it," he said.

"She looks like Madonna on too many steroids," I said.

He seemed to like this idea.

"I've got to go," I snapped, getting off the bike.

"Hey, Dime — c'mon," he called.

I turned around. There was that forever hope again, like a quick song in my chest. Maybe I was wrong. Maybe I was jumping to too many conclusions.

"Come here. Please?" He had on his take-you-out-of-deep-freeze smile. I hesitated, then walked back, pretending to be reluctant. Truth was, my heart was slam-dancing against my chest. I wanted him to like me so bad.

"Hey," he said softly and touched my face. Then he kissed me. Well, that was that — he took me up to cloud nine and we stayed there for a while. Finally, he put on his helmet and roared off. I stood and stared after him. I didn't know if I was coming or going with him. He just twisted and turned me all over the place.

When I got into the apartment, the phone was ringing. It was Mom, wanting to know about every detail of my love life. So I hung up on her. Then I made hamburgers again for supper, but Darren didn't complain. We watched *Old Yeller* on TV while we ate. It made me cry. I sat there sniffing into my T-shirt sleeve as the dog died. Then I looked over at Darren and saw that his eyes were red too.

"Why are you crying?" I asked.

"Why are you?" he shrugged. He headed off to the bathroom and I followed. Darren never cries.

"I'm weeping buckets because the dog died," I said.

"Sure," said Darren. He was taking his laxative. He takes it three times a week so he can take a dump the next morning. It's part of being a quad, just like using a leg bag to pee. Darren can change his own leg bag, but I still hate thinking about it.

"You're feeling sorry for me," Darren said.

"No, I'm not," I said.

Darren looked right at me and said, "Yes, you are. Listen, Dime — my life is going a hundred times better than yours.

I'm halfway through my engineering degree. You're close to flunking Grade 10."

I get mad fast. When I do, my brain flies into a hundred pieces. I turned to leave the room.

"No one will ever hire you," I said.

Behind me, Darren's voice just got louder. He said, "They'd hire me before they'd hire you. And when they do, I'll be making sixty grand a year. You'll be flipping hamburgers for the rest of your life."

That was when I really lost it. The last person I could take coming down on me was Darren.

I yelled, "At least I can do that. You need help to go to the can."

"So I have to park my butt on that toilet two hours tomorrow morning and wait. At least I'm getting rid of the crap in my life. You're keeping yours bottled up inside, Dime. You don't even know what's bugging you," Darren yelled.

Darren's apartment was too small. There was nowhere to go to get away from him. I walked quickly to the kitchen, but he zipped after me. He was actually chasing me in his chair! I leaned my face against the cool fridge door and closed my eyes.

"Sure I do. I don't go on about it, but I do," I said.

"So talk about it. Tell me what it is. Don't just bawl at old movies," Darren said softly.

But I couldn't. I turned away, ending the conversation. For the rest of the evening, Darren studied in his room. I watched TV.

Chapter Six

Tuesday morning when I got up, Darren's aide was just coming in. I rushed through my bathroom routine, then headed for the kitchen. As Darren wheeled into the bathroom, I pretended to be watching the toast in the toaster.

"Good morning, Dime," he said.

"Yeah," I said.

Everywhere I looked, trouble was building. I didn't want to think about Gabe's ex waiting for me at school. I didn't want to think about the way Gabe grinned when he saw her. And I knew I couldn't stand one more raging phone call from Mom or Dad. So I pretended to water the plant on the counter and soaked the phone instead. It would dry out in a week or so. In the meantime, there would be no more nagging phone calls.

Gabe had promised to give me a driving lesson before school. I smeared honey onto my toast and shoved it into my mouth. Then I headed out the door. I was early, so I sat on the curb. But even though I wanted to, I couldn't stop my head from working. I kept seeing the stack of *Reader's Digest* magazines that Darren keeps by the toilet. He reads them while he waits for his laxative to work. How could he keep everything going in his life when I couldn't? I might as well have FAILURE tattooed across my forehead.

Gabe roared up with his usual grin. Instead of getting on behind him, I got on in front and faced him.

"Take off your helmet," I said. We made out for a bit. Gabe could be really good at helping me take my mind off things.

"You're in a good mood," he mumbled.

"Yeah," I said.

Gabe let me drive once we were outside Winnipeg. I was doing fine — I even remembered the brakes when I needed them. Gabe's hands were resting around my waist instead of hanging on as if I was about to crash. So I relaxed, and that was when the problem kicked in. Suddenly, I started to hear my parents' voices inside my head.

You're such a disappointment to us, Dime, said Mom.

Why can't you grow up and act your age? yelled Dad. Then he sighed. *You know, we really love you. If you could only see how much we love you.*

I blinked, trying to concentrate. The road had disappeared. I felt a sharp drop, and then we were driving over something bumpy. Gabe was yelling and banging his helmet against the back of mine again. That was when I saw I'd driven off the road and was headed across a field. But I remembered the brake and got us stopped.

Gabe was off the bike in a second and grabbing at the handles. Maybe he was afraid I wanted to do wheelies in the field.

"You're crazy! You're nuts! Get off my bike!" he howled.

I got off. Then I decided to pretend I'd been trying to miss a rabbit hopping across the road.

"Did you see that rabbit? Did you see that rabbit?" I asked, pointing at a thick bush.

"What rabbit?" Gabe asked slowly.

"I saw this rabbit going across the road and it scared me. It was a white rabbit," I lied.

"There was no rabbit! Give me my helmet!" Gabe yelled.

I gave it to him. Then he was gone, roaring across the field and down the road. This time I didn't wait for him to come back — I figured the helmet was pretty final. It took me forty minutes to get back into the city.

Then it was a twenty-five-minute bus ride to school. All the way, my parents' voices kept going inside my head.

I came out of the school office with a late slip and a detention. I was pretty upset about the detention. My late slips had been adding up, but it was Gabe's fault I was late. I figured he should be the one getting the detention. But at least the hallways were empty, and I could walk without looking over my shoulder. And with classes on, the ex wouldn't be camped out at my locker.

Halfway through science class, the fire alarm went off. Usually a fire alarm break is fun, but we were in the middle of an experiment. We turned off the Bunsen burners and headed out. Up and down the hall, guys were jumping up and popping out ceiling tiles. Tiff came up beside me.

"Did you hear?" she asked.

"About what?" I asked.

"Your big showdown with the ex."

"Tell me where to be. And when." I didn't want to fight, but I couldn't seem to make myself care anymore. When I get that way, my mouth becomes a problem.

"The ex has invited another school to watch," Tiff warned.

"Is she selling tickets? Is it winner take all?" I asked. We were coming out into the back parking lot. I could see Gabe sitting on his bike, his fans all around him. The fire alarm was still going.

"Dime, this is serious," said Tiff.

"Life is serious, but you can turn it into one big joke if you have to," I said.

Gabe waved and called, "Dime!"

For a second I thought about going over and slashing his tires. But it passed. I *had* driven his bike onto a farmer's field, after all. I should consider myself lucky, really, that he'd gotten over it. So I walked over to him, smiling. He put an arm around me.

"You made it back. I was worried," he said. He looked concerned about me.

"I'm okay. Sorry I drove you off the road," I said.

"I went back looking for you," he said.

Part of me wanted to believe him. But the road back to Winnipeg had been pretty straight. How could I have missed a guy on a motorcycle? That was when I noticed the ex nearby, looking straight at us. Gabe glanced at her and grinned. At the same time, he tightened his arm around my shoulder. It felt like a trap.

"Too bad you didn't bring the ex with you this morning. She could have knocked me off and buried me in one of those fields," I said, pulling back.

"Hey, Dime, you're the love of my life. Don't be mad at me," Gabe said softly. Then he pulled me in against him. I buried my face in his neck and tried to forget about the ex. Maybe Gabe wasn't Mr. Perfect, but he sure looked like him. And he could hand out pretty good hugs. This one would be enough to keep me going until lunch, when I could find him again. I hung onto him tightly until the alarm went off, and everyone headed back into the school.

Chapter Seven

At lunch break, I stuck close to Gabe. I figured the ex wasn't going to try and pull me off his body, and she didn't. Maybe the whole thing was nothing more than rumors. At any rate, I was still in one piece when I got home that afternoon. I decided to try something more complicated than hamburgers for supper — fish and chips. I knew Darren liked them.

"Got a lot of homework tonight?" Darren asked after supper.

This was a parent-type question. My smile faded. "No," I shrugged.

"There's a good band playing near here. Get it done and we'll go," he said.

"Serious?" I asked.

"My thank-you for a superb supper," he grinned.

Darren hadn't noticed that the phone had died. With no one calling to interrupt me, I actually finished my homework. Well, maybe not exactly *finished*, but as much as I could handle in one sitting. If I was going to catch up on all the homework I'd missed, I'd be there for weeks.

At 9 p.m., Darren and I headed out to his favorite bar. Some of his friends were there and we joined them at a table. Another guy at the table was also in a wheelchair.

"He got arrested for drunk driving. He was going down the middle of the road in his chair," Darren whispered.

"Are any of you quads normal people?" I joked.

Darren shrugged. "What's normal?"

As usual, some of the crowd couldn't

seem to stop watching the wheelchairs. People are always surprised to see someone in a wheelchair having a good time. It's as if they think life in a wheelchair is only good for watching TV. One woman came by and patted Darren's arm.

"I wanted to tell you I think you're so brave. I'm sure you'll get well some day," she said, her voice wobbling.

"But I am well," Darren said.

As she walked away, he made a face at me. "No one can believe I might actually enjoy life these days," he said.

"So, she's stupid," I said.

"A lot of people are like that," he said.

"I'd trade places with you any day. I want to be you more than anything," I said. Then I sat staring at my pop. I couldn't believe I'd finally said it to him.

Darren pushed his beer bottle around the table in small circles. Then he said softly, "I'm not always crazy about my life, Dime. I don't talk about it much. You're right — I cry at sad movies instead. Sometimes I read the entire *TV Guide* to find a movie that will let me cry the longest."

He tried to smile, but it didn't quite work. I hate it when my brother gets sad. I get scared for him, and this huge hurt shoots right through me. My next thoughts burst out of my mouth.

"It should have happened to me. I'm the loser. If I'd broken my neck, it wouldn't have been such a waste. I used to wish it happened to me. After the accident, I even prayed about it. 'Dear God, please put me in a wheelchair, so Darren can be alive again.'"

The words pulled themselves out of somewhere deep inside me. I guess I'd been hiding them down there for a long time. When I finished speaking, I felt really tired, as if I'd been working hard all day.

"Dime, you're worse than that woman. I'm not dead!" said Darren.

"Might as well be," I said softly.

"Is that why you want to be me — so you can be half-dead?" asked Darren.

"No, because you can handle things.

You don't mess up all the time. Mom and Dad love you," I pointed out.

"Do you really want to get along with them?" asked Darren.

Suddenly, it hit me so hard — an old wish that my parents and I could sit in the same room and be happy together. Sometimes I had dreams of sitting at the kitchen table just talking to them. We were laughing, telling jokes. Mom patted my arm. Dad said, "You're such a fine girl, Dime."

But I couldn't tell Darren this, so I shrugged and said, "Maybe. Yeah. If they'd stop yelling."

"D'you think if you stopped trying to put yourself in a wheelchair, they'd stop yelling? One quad per family is enough," said Darren.

"They were like this before your accident. They've always liked you better," I said.

Darren didn't argue. He frowned and said, "I've always hated that. I wish I knew how to change it, but I don't. Maybe you're right about them being afraid of you. Even way back when you were seven or eight."

"Yeah, but why?" I asked.

"You're different. You like music that sounds like a gravel truck. You'd rather smash through a wall than use a door. I'm more like them," Darren said.

"You are not," I said, rolling my eyes.

Darren grinned and said, "Put it to you this way, Dime. They'd like you more if you were like them. But it would cost you. For one thing, you'd have to dress like them. I do. But then, I like it."

Tonight, my brother was dressed like a preppie. I was trying hard to ignore this.

Darren kept talking. He seemed to have an awful lot to say tonight. Leaning forward, he said, "I think because you're so different, they get confused. More than confused — they're scared for you. You're always pushing the edge. Remember when I first came home from the hospital? You got suspended from school just so you could be with me. We watched the soaps all week. I never felt closer to anyone. That meant a lot."

"Yeah," I said, looking away. It was a tough week to remember.

Darren touched my hand and said softly, "You almost flunked your year because of that. But you can't keep wrecking your life to prove that you love me, Dime."

I stared at him. "What d'you mean?"

Darren's face grew sad. As he stared at his curled-up fingers, he said, "It hurts me to think about the accident and what I lost. It hurts a lot. But it's my pain, Dime — not yours. When you go around hurting yourself, you don't help me. I know it means we both hurt at the same time, but that makes it worse for me. I love my little sister. That means I want her to do well. That would make me feel like a million bucks."

Darren smiled, then added, "And it doesn't mean you have to dress like me."

"So what does it mean?" I asked.

Darren paused. Then he asked, "What d'you like about Gabe?"

That wasn't hard.

"His bod. And his bike," I grinned.

"D'you like the way he treats you?" Darren asked.

Okay, so now we were getting to the tough questions. I tried to shrug this one off. With a bored face, I asked, "What do you mean?"

Darren shrugged back, then said, "Ordering you around. Turning on our stereo without asking."

Opening the fridge without asking too, I thought. I knew Darren must be getting close to his punch line. This conversation was moving along too easily, as if he'd been planning it for a while. But it didn't feel like a set-up to me. It felt like he cared.

"So?" I asked, kind of tough.

Darren took a deep breath and said slowly, "What's the difference between the way Gabe treats you, and the way Mom and Dad do?"

I felt as if he'd picked up his beer bottle and whacked me with it. My face got hot. Then I tried for a joke, but it was pretty weak.

"C'mon, what about his bod and his bike? And the way he dresses?" I asked.

"You can get a bod with a better attitude," Darren smiled.

"What about a bike?" I grinned weakly.

Now that we were through the tough stuff, Darren lit up like the sun. He beamed at me and said, "Y'know my friend Larry? He'll teach you to drive his bike. He's got a Harley with a sidecar. And he knows about a used Kawasaki Ninja I can get dirt cheap. You get your license, and I'll buy it for you. Then you and Larry and I will take a trip this summer. Larry can be my aide."

Excitement blazed through me.

"Where can we go?" I demanded.

"How about California?" Darren asked.

"Wow! You mean it?" I shouted.

"Yes," Darren grinned.

"So you're saying if I dump Gabe, and get along with Mom and Dad —" I started.

Darren frowned, then said, "No,

that's your business. But if you complain about Mom and Dad, why not Gabe?"

"Y'know, I think he actually wants me to fight his ex to prove that I love him," I said quietly. I felt so stupid having to admit this to my brother.

"If he really cared about you, would he want that?" Darren asked.

I guess that was the question to ask. And the answer was pretty obvious. *No*. Or, as Gabe would have put it: *No, no, no*.

Then Darren asked, "And if you really loved yourself, would you do it?"

It was another good question, with another obvious answer. I figured — change the subject. So I asked, "Hey, d'you think Mom and Dad would come over for supper some night? If I didn't make hamburgers?"

Darren laughed.

"Except we'd have to get a new phone to call them. I sort of drowned your old one while I was watering the plants," I admitted.

"I already bought one. You owe me forty bucks," Darren said.

Chapter Eight

The next morning, I had to fight my way out of my blankets, but I made it. There really was no choice — the night before, I'd put my radio on the other side of the room. Then I'd turned it to a country station. I hate country, but I knew it would force me to get up when the alarm went off. Someone was howling, "Baby, baby, the full moon rises in your eyes." I would have crawled out of my grave to shut that guy off.

Darren looked pretty beat too. His aide was in the kitchen, helping him get ready for an early class. As I tore past him and out the door, I waved madly. I'd already missed the early bus, but I reached the stop in time for the next one. I spent the entire ride waiting at the back door. When the bus reached the school, the late bell was ringing. I pushed open the door and hit the ground running. I was lucky. My homeroom teacher gave me a break, probably because I was breathing so hard. I was so relieved I didn't get sent to the office for another late slip. I already had a major collection. I'll have to remember the breathing-hard trick for the next time.

Halfway through my first class, I realized I hadn't seen Gabe yet. Then I realized that our phone had been working the night before and he hadn't called. I didn't worry too much about it though. My math class was actually kind of interesting — finishing homework helps, I guess. But at mid-morning break, something happened to make me think about Gabe for the rest of the morning. I was walking down the hall toward science class, when I passed a girls' bathroom. The door was open, and I could see girls crowded inside. They were standing on tiptoe.

"Fight, fight," they were saying.

The weird thing was how quiet they all were. I guess no one wanted a teacher coming in. There were all kinds of girls in there — preppies, skaters, jocks and headbangers. No one was stopping the fight — they all wanted it to go on as long as possible. It was like a show to them, something to watch on TV.

I stood at the back of the crowd, wondering what to do. No one likes do-gooders at our school. I wouldn't be making myself popular if I tried to help. The bathroom was packed and the fight was going on by the sinks. I couldn't see who was fighting because of the crowd, and I didn't know why they were fighting. Maybe the girl going down had asked for it. On the other hand, maybe the Queen of the Cans was taking down some poor loser.

Whatever, I shrugged. It wasn't my problem, and I already had enough to deal with.

But a new thought stopped me from walking away. What if it had been me in there getting hammered? The ex was just waiting for the right time and place. Would anyone help me when she jumped me? Of course not — I knew that answer without having to ask the question. So if I walked away from this fight, was I any better than the girls who were watching it?

I stood thinking about it too long. The fight was over by the time I began pushing my way into the crowd. I never even saw who the winner was. Girls were rushing out of the bathroom to tell the rest of the school about the fight. Only one girl was left behind, standing by the sinks. She looked familiar, but she was older than me. I didn't know her name. Her nose was bleeding a little, and there were scratches on her arms. She smelled as if she'd been drinking.

"You all right?" I asked.

She didn't even look at me. At our school, it isn't cool to ask that kind of question. Without a word, she pushed past me and walked out. I stared into the mirror and imagined blood pouring from my nose. Had this fight been over a guy? Was he worth it? I tried to imagine slamming my fist into the ex's nose and scratching her arms. Was Gabe worth that? Was any guy?

Science class went by in a blur while I thought and thought. Finally the bell rang. I pushed my way through the crowded halls, still thinking. When I got to my locker, I found Tiff waiting for me.

"You're not going to be happy when we get outside," she warned.

"Why not?" I asked, shoving my books into my locker.

"You'll see," she sighed.

"C'mon Tiff — don't do this to me," I begged, but she wouldn't tell me. We headed out the back door, and I caught on pretty fast. You have to when the reason is mashed in your face. There was Gabe's ex, sitting on his bike with her arms wrapped around him. Gabe was grinning as if he was starring in a toothpaste commercial.

So now she's the ex-ex, I thought. *That's why Gabe didn't call last night.*

"He changes his mind like he changes his underwear," Tiff muttered.

Gabe saw me. His grin got a little wider, and he lifted an eyebrow. Then he looked away. I felt like something that had been thrown into the trash. For a moment, I considered creeping off to my library hideout. Then I remembered what Darren had said about Gabe ordering me around. Gabe wasn't actually saying anything right now. Still, he was telling me, *I'm finished with you, so get lost.*

Well, I was finished with him too.

The thought blew through me like a happy wind, cleaning out a lot of crud. I realized I was actually relieved to see the whole thing end. Everything with Gabe had been so confusing. I never knew when he was about to blow up. From the beginning, I'd always felt as if he was about to ditch me. Suddenly I realized he'd wanted me to feel that way. He'd wanted me to feel so low-down that I'd do anything to keep him.

I took a deep, thinking breath. You had to be pretty insecure to treat other people that way. Sometime real soon I was going to go looking for a bod with a better attitude. But that didn't mean I had to be mean to Gabe. Or to his ex-ex. Well, okay — she has a name. It's Lena.

I walked up to them and leaned against the bike. Everyone around us tuned in as if this was prime-time TV.

"Hi, Gabe. Hi, Lena," I said.

Gabe lost half his grin. I could tell he was nervous. I wasn't running off the way I was supposed to.

"Get lost," Lena said.

"I wanted to wish you the best," I said.

"I said, get lost," said Lena. Maybe she thought I was a germ and Gabe might catch me again. She got off the bike and stood staring at me. Yup, she looked hostile.

"Hey, relax. I left my brass knuckles and chains at home," I said.

Lena stepped forward and pushed me hard. I bumped into Tiff, who bumped into someone else, who kept us standing up. This was helpful, because I had to duck a couple of swings Lena took at me. Gabe sat and watched as if one of his dreams was coming true — two girls fighting for his love.

No, Gabe, Lena's the only one fighting for you, I thought. I stepped back. Lena stopped swinging and waited to see what I'd do.

I looked at Lena's face. Even with the killer look she was wearing, she was pretty. But for the first time, I saw how sad she was. She didn't like herself much. She was fighting for Gabe because she thought he was all she could get.

Gabe knew this, and he'd use it to get what he wanted from her. All the kids watching and cheering probably knew it too. But Lena had to figure it out for herself, just like I had.

In spite of everything, I wanted to kiss Gabe goodbye. But I didn't. Instead I said, "Lena, he's yours."

Then I turned and walked away.

Chapter Nine

"C'mon, babe, give me another chance. It was just a one-day thing with Lena," said Gabe.

It was two days after the parking lot showdown. I sat in our kitchen and stared at the phone. When I'd first heard Gabe's voice on the other end, I'd felt so happy. Then I'd started to feel like a pretzel, all twisted around.

"Maybe I'll be another one-day thing for you too," I said.

"No, babe. Never you," Gabe said quickly.

"I don't want to go out with you anymore," I said.

Then I hung up the phone. It felt as if I was hanging up on my heart. You can make a decision with your head. It still takes your heart a while to catch up with it. For the next few weeks, I thought about Gabe a lot. There were bad moments, when I remembered his grin and his bod. And there was that bike. I spent a solid week watching my wall blur as the tears came. But slowly the lump in my stomach faded. It was May, and that beautiful green thing was happening to the trees. I had a ton of homework I needed to catch up on. And final exams were one month away.

Final exams! I wasn't used to studying, and it was hard to get into. I had to psyche myself up for it. I'd stand at one end of my room and take a run at the opposite wall. As my shoulder hit, I'd yell, "I hate this! I hate this!" After a couple of minutes of this, I was ready to sit down and work. Darren got used to it. I think my general problem is that

I need to make a lot of noise. Let me do that, and I'm fine.

Darren's friend Larry started taking me for lessons on his Harley. He had a pretty good bod. Better than that, he never yelled. It took me a while to realize he wasn't going to blow up if I made a mistake. When I finally figured this out, I stopped blanking out. It made me one heck of a better driver — at least now I stayed on the road.

I also realized that the reason I blanked out was because I was afraid of being yelled at. I'd always thought it was because I was crazy, a loner or just plain stupid. I'd never realized it was fear. I tried to figure out what exactly I was afraid of. Finally, I realized I was afraid of not being good enough. The fear had started way back when I was small, and it hadn't gone away when I got older. The blanking out had always been there, right along with the fear.

Blanking out is when Nothing drops on you. It's the feeling of The Big Nothing. It used to drop on me a lot when I lived with my parents. Now I'd finally figured out what it meant — if Mom and Dad didn't love me, then I was nothing. That was the way I'd always felt around my parents. When you feel like nothing, you treat yourself like nothing. You let other people treat you like nothing too.

But Darren had said that Mom and Dad were afraid of me too. Maybe he was right. They sounded angry, but maybe most of their anger was pain, like mine. Did I want all my time with my parents to be like the past — full of hurting and yelling? They'd never slapped me around or anything like that. I started to wonder if this was a family that could be fixed.

So, on the last Saturday in May, I picked up the phone and called my parents. It felt strange. Since I'd left, they'd called me but I hadn't called them once. I got Dad, halfway through reading the morning paper.

"Dime?" he said. His voice had a funny wobble in it.

I mumbled, "Dad. I was wondering..."

Suddenly, I didn't know what to say. When you need it the most, English seems to turn into a foreign language.

"Yes?" he asked after a long pause.

"Would you and Mom like to come over for supper? I promise I won't make hamburgers," I said quickly. I knew I had to get off the phone fast. My brain was headed for a major blank.

"How about tonight?" he asked.

"Tonight?" I squeaked. This was going too fast. I'd been thinking maybe Christmas, so I could work up to it.

"We're free tonight," said Dad, sounding excited.

I swallowed. Tonight.

"Um, okay," I said.

"We'll bring dessert," he said cheerfully and hung up.

Darren and I worked all afternoon on macaroni and cheese. He figured out the recipe while I did the hard labour. It was lucky he was in charge of the thinking part, because I kept blanking out. Just before five, I looked at him and said, "My stomach hurts."

"What are you worried about?" Darren asked.

What was the first thing? I wondered.

"Should I take out my nose ring?" I asked.

"D'you like wearing it?" Darren asked.

"Yes," I said.

"Then wear it," he shrugged.

The buzzer went at 5:30. I opened the door. My parents stepped in and stood there as if they were afraid to move. *They are afraid,* I thought. *Afraid this isn't going to work.*

I didn't step forward and give them a Walt Disney hug and kiss. But I took their coats and hung them up — even in May, my parents wear coats. Mom had brought an apple pie and ice cream. With a nervous smile, she asked if she could put the ice cream into the fridge. It made me think of Gabe. And seeing how nervous they were made me less nervous. After all, they were visitors in my home!

"Sure, Mom," I smiled.

They didn't stare at my nose ring, though they took a few runs at it with their eyes. And they sure perked up when I told them I was studying. They even handled the bike lessons with Larry all right. *Who are these people?* I thought. *Surely not my parents!*

But then, I wasn't yelling at them either. They were probably wondering when I'd had the brain transplant.

"Would you like more coffee?" I asked, standing up.

Dad looked at me and smiled. Suddenly his eyes were getting red, as if he was about to cry.

"Could you sit down a minute, please, Dime?" he asked.

My heart started going like a heavy metal concert. I sat.

"Dime, we want you to move back home," Dad said.

Mom played with her wedding ring. "The house is so quiet without you," she said.

"Maybe we could figure out something that would work for all of us. A 9 p.m. curfew is too early on Fridays," Dad said.

"We just wanted to make sure you passed Grade 10," Mom added.

"I am passing," I said. *Without a curfew*, I added to myself.

"But you weren't before," Mom said quickly.

"Y'know why?" I asked.

My chin went up and I looked her in the eye. Mom blinked but she kept looking at me.

"Why?" she asked quietly.

"I wondered what you'd do if I flunked out," I said.

Mom looked as if I'd hit her. So did Dad.

"Or what you'd do if I wore a nose ring. Or if I dated Gabe," I went on. Things were making more and more sense as I talked.

Mom and Dad glanced at each other, then down. They were actually listening to me!

"I figured you were looking for a reason to kick me out. You seemed so tired of me all the time," I said.

"We didn't kick you out. Darren offered his place for a while. Until you worked things out," Dad said.

I stared at Darren in shock. Was *he* going to kick me out now — back to Mom and Dad?

"That's not what I said, Dad. I said Dime could come and live with me. And that's for good, if she wants to. I'd like that," said Darren. He smiled at me.

Tears stung my eyes. I took a deep breath and smiled back. I couldn't have handled it if Darren had said he was sending me back to Mom and Dad. But he hadn't. He'd said this was my home.

It felt like home.

"You sound as if you think we hate you," Mom said. She played with her coffee cup.

"We don't hate you," Dad added quickly.

It was a far cry from saying "We love you," but I guess that doesn't come quickly. At least we could sit at the same table now and talk — without yelling.

"I like living with Darren. I'm doing okay here. I'm making good decisions," I said.

"And she's a great cook," Darren said. I'd made chili the night before.

"But we're your parents — you should live with your parents," Mom said.

"I don't want to get rid of you. I still want my Mom and Dad. But this is where I'm doing okay — with my brother. I want to stay here," I said.

There was a long pause while Mom and Dad stared at the wall.

"Well, you do seem to be doing better. And Darren has company now," Dad said finally.

"And Dime's a great cook!" Darren repeated.

"You will come to visit? And talk to us on the phone?" Mom asked.

"If you take me out for dinner on my birthday," I grinned weakly.

Everyone smiled then. It was a smile with some sadness. I guess we realized we'd never be the picture-perfect family. But there were other ways of getting along. Maybe we could find what worked for us.

Chapter Ten

Well, I did it — passed everything, though math came in at fifty-three percent. And when I got an A on my driver's exam, my parents looked relieved. Mom even got on the back of the secondhand Kawasaki Ninja that Darren bought me. Then I drove her up and down the alley. She just about cut off my air hanging onto me. When I suggested she come along on our trip, she went white and leaned against the fence. It was a major blank for her. Twenty kilometers per hour on the back of a bike was a big step.

Then I took Dad for a spin. He wanted to ride all over, even out of the city — at the speed limit. When I brought him back, he took off the helmet I'd loaned him, and handed it to me. The hair he combs over his bald spot stood up with excitement. He got all stiff for a moment. Then he pushed his hand toward me. It landed on my shoulder like a grenade.

"Dime, you're a good driver. I'm proud of you," he said.

A smile cut through my face. It had been so long since I'd smiled — really smiled — around my parents. It just about wrecked my face.

"Thanks, Dad," I beamed.

I practiced driving around with Larry and my brother. Darren rode in Larry's sidecar. At first, he wanted to stop every five minutes to look at this and that. It was like taking your grandmother to a garage sale. Darren kept pointing at everything and rocking in his seat, taking a hairy if I kept going.

"Darren, if you do this on our trip, we'll never get to California," I complained.

He thought this was a great joke. "Just drive a little closer to those blue flowers," he grinned.

Darren is really into plants ... and opening bottles with his teeth. That's my engineer brother!

My sixteenth birthday came the last week of school. Mom and Dad took Darren, Tiff and me out for dinner. They gave me a helmet called a Skull Cap. After dinner, I loaded Tiff onto the back of the Ninja, and we left the family behind. I'd passed my license that afternoon and it was my first time driving alone. We cruised Winnipeg for hours and dropped in on a few house parties. Not for long, though. I'd get to a party and all I'd want to do was stare out the window at my bike. Tiff finally got tired of cruising, so I took off on my own. There I was — just me and the road and the huge night sky. Sixteen was going to be one great year!

Darren and I finally got our things packed for California. Mom and Dad stood next to Tiff to watch us roar out of the parking lot. By now, we could hug and kiss and say "I love you" again. It felt good. My whole life felt good.

Dad hugged me. Then he said, "Now, you listen to Darren. He's your older brother."

I got stiff.

Dad grinned at Darren. "Now, you listen to your sister. She knows how to drive and cook."

Darren and I both laughed.

"We're looking forward to you coming back," Mom told me. Then she even tugged on my nose ring!

Driving out of the city, I was on such a high. I think I was traveling faster than the bike. Then I saw a 7-Eleven up ahead. I signaled to Larry and Darren and pulled into the parking lot. A group of kids was sitting around Gabe's bike, admiring his biceps. Larry pulled his Harley up beside me. As I took off my Skull Cap, Gabe's eyes bugged.

"Hi," I grinned.

"Awk," he said.

"Just wanted to wish you a good summer," I said.

"Huh?" he asked.

"We're on our way to California. Right, Darren?" I asked my brother.

"Right, Dime," he replied.

I put my Skull Cap back on. My life sure had changed. I could have been spending the summer in this parking lot with Gabe, going nowhere. But now I had better things to do. I reached over and touched Darren's hand.

"Thanks," I said.

And then, we were off.